A book is a curious thing.

Inside, you might find short tales or long chronicles
or some stories that never really end at all.

And some books, though entirely made up, are absolutely
true—giving us the power to see what could be instead of
what is, to shape tomorrows before they become yesterdays.

And who knows how the world might change because of it.

Published 2021

THE TRUTH about *Stories*

WRITTEN BY **Leah Byrd**

ILLUSTRATED BY **Samantha Rapp**

Each evening, as the first lightning bug blinks awake,
the library begins to stir.

And if you happen to be walking east
down a rarely traveled road
you just might see it tucked behind the trees.

Inside, **the fluttering pages** whisper of fairy tales and sea monsters...

of white rabbits and hot air balloons, and adventures that stretch across oceans and centuries.

Wandering down hallways,
   and up around stairways,
   room after room...

Each doorway
   (unlike the doorway to your neighbor's house
      or your favorite ice cream shop)
   leads you to worlds
      that are quite unlike
         the one you sit in now.

In the circus room,

the smell of caramel popcorn
mingles with the smell of old books.

And if you arrive before the lions finish
their afternoon nap, you might catch
a glimpse of Eloise the Elephant
practicing her opening act.

In the pirate room,

which contains every swashbuckling, seafaring tale
ever to be spoken or written,
a ship with bright sails
floats across a shadowy sea.

You could spend hours
exploring the boughs and hedges
of the **enchanted** forest room.

Or nestle up in the clouds of the sky room

tracing one **constellation**

after the next.

You might find yourself in a **lively debate**
about plankton migration with a salt river mermaid
or having afternoon tea
with a bashful Western Canopy dragon.

You could meet a 12th-century explorer
or an 18th-century inventor,
a penguin-training poet
or a souffle-baking painter.

You may discover short tales
and long chronicles
and some stories that
never really end at all,
but ripple and overlap,
weaving into one another
until there is no way to tell
where one story ends
and another begins.

You might find that some tales evolve over time...

...changing and growing alongside you.

You might find that some characters
become close friends and
stay with you
long after the book has closed.

ORIENTATION

You may discover that there are **facts**
and there are **truths...**

...and that sometimes the difference
is difficult to define.

Some books have rows and rows of facts
carefully stacked and organized to ensure
no nonsense or folly slips through.

Filled with dates and graphs and
documented evidence,
these books can teach you how rockets fly
or how to fix your toaster
or how Albert Einstein met Marie Curie.

But truths are trickier.

They're not facts, and they're not **NOT** facts.
They're... **MORE** than facts.

They reach further and burrow deeper...

...revealing all the ways **we're connected** despite all the things that separate us.

Some books
   though entirely made up
   are absolutely true.

They teach us about **hopes**
   and **fears**
      and **joys**
         and **disappointments.**

In these pages, people who never existed
teach us how life can be experienced
in so many different ways.

Some stories are truer than fact,
and that is their **magic.**

That magic is passed on to the reader,

giving them the power to see what could be
instead of what is,
to shape tomorrows
before they become yesterdays.

And who knows how the world might change
because of it.

So, if you happen to be walking east
down a rarely traveled road
as the first lightning bug blinks awake,
take a closer look...

Some stories are true, after all.

Made in the USA
Las Vegas, NV
07 May 2021